Leif

HENRY

JAMES

PERCY

First published 1992 by Buzz Books,
an imprint of Reed International Books Ltd
Michelin House, 81 Fulham Road, London SW3 6RB

LONDON MELBOURNE AUCKLAND

ISBN 1 85591 246 5

Printed and bound in Great Britain by BPCC Hazell Books,
Paulton and Aylesbury

THOMAS, PERCY AND THE POST TRAIN

buzz books

At night, when the other engines are tucked away in their sheds, you can still hear the faraway call of an engine's whistle and the clickety-clack of train wheels turning.

This is the sound of the post train.

One train is pulled by Thomas and the other by Percy, as the loads are too heavy for one engine to do the work alone.

The post is loaded into trucks at both the harbours and the engines pull their trains through the silent stations delivering their precious loads.

On a clear night, a big shiny moon brightens their journey, but often Thomas and Percy can't even see the stars!

But whatever the weather, lamps
along the track always light their way.

One night Percy was waiting at the junction.

The main line train was late.

At last Henry arrived. "Sorry," he puffed.
"The mail boat from the mainland was
delayed."

"Come on, Percy," said his driver.
"Let's make up for lost time."

Percy puffed along as quickly as he could, but the sun was already rising as he finished his work.

"Never mind," thought Percy. "It's nice to be up and about when it's the start of a new day and there's no-one else around."

Percy was not alone for long.

"Bother," said Percy. "It's that dizzy thing, Harold."

"Good morning," whirred Harold. "I always said railways were out of date, but you're so slow with the post, you should give everyone their stamps back post haste!"

Percy was too tired to explain.
"Bird brain," he muttered.

"Good morning, Percy," called Duck. "You're up early."

"No, you're wrong," sighed Percy. "I'm back, tired and late."

He rolled into the shed and fell asleep almost before his buffers touched the bar.

His driver decided to set off early that evening.

Thomas was waiting at the station.

"Thank goodness I've a chance to speak to you. Driver says that the person in charge of the post has complained to the Fat Controller about the delay last night."

20

"But that wasn't my fault," replied Percy.

"I know," said Thomas. "And so does the
Fat Controller, but this post person
wouldn't listen. Tonight we'll just have to
be quicker than ever before."

21

The engines were just leaving the station when they heard a familiar buzzing.

"I say, you two, there's news flying about."

"Where?" puffed Percy.

"All over the place. They're going to scrap the post train and use me instead. Wings work wonders, you know, always."

"Rubbish," huffed Thomas.

That night, everything ran like clockwork. Thomas and Percy steamed through the stations making good time everywhere they went.

At a station, Thomas noticed a man looking cold and worried. He had missed his train home.

"We can give you a ride," said Thomas's driver. "But it will be rather uncomfortable."

"Thank you," said the man. "Anything's better than sitting here."

The next afternoon Percy passed the
airfield and saw Harold.

"Hello, Lazywings. Are you too tired to
fly today?"

"The wind's too strong. I've been grounded," grumbled Harold.

"You need rails," laughed Percy. "They work wonders, you know — always!"

That night the Fat Controller showed the two engines a letter. It was from the man who had missed his train.

"He thinks you are both splendid," said the Fat Controller, "and everyone says that the post train is the pride of the line!"

THOMAS

EDWARD

GORDON